DAREDEVIL PARK

BY SARA AND SPENCER COMPTON

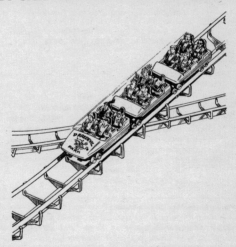

ILLUSTRATED BY FRANK BOLLE

An Edward Packard Book

BANTAM BOOKS®

NEW YORK • TORONTO • LONDON • SYDNEY • AUCKLAND

RL 4, age 10 and up

DAREDEVIL PARK

A Bantam Book / June 1991

*CHOOSE YOUR OWN ADVENTURE® is a registered trademark of
Bantam Books, a division of Bantam Doubleday Dell Publishing
Group, Inc. Registered in U.S. Patent and Trademark Office
and elsewhere.*

Original conception of Edward Packard

Cover art by Catherine Huerta
Interior illustrations by Frank Bolle

ISBN 0-553-28795-8

Published simultaneously in the United States and Canada

*Bantam Books are published by Bantam Books, a division of Bantam
Doubleday Dell Publishing Group, Inc. Its trademark, consisting of the
words "Bantam Books" and the portrayal of a rooster, is Registered in U.S.
Patent and Trademark Office and in other countries. Marca Registrada.
Bantam Books, 1540 Broadway, New York, New York 10036.*

PRINTED IN THE UNITED STATES OF AMERICA

OPM   12 11 10 9 8 7 6 5

DAREDEVIL PARK

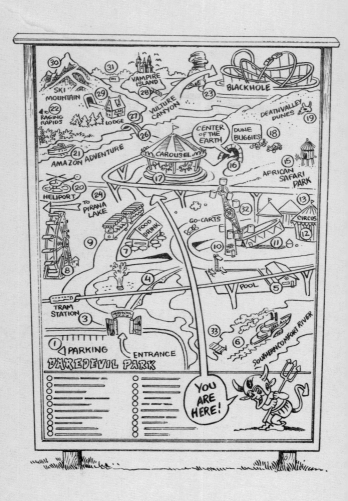

WARNING!!!

Do not read this book straight through from beginning to end. These pages contain many different adventures that you may have when you win a free trip to Daredevil Park. From time to time as you read along, you will be asked to make a choice. Your choice may lead to success or disaster!

The adventures you have are the results of your choices. You are responsible because you choose! After you make a choice, follow the instructions to find out what happens to you next.

Think carefully before you make a decision. Amusement parks can be fun, but Daredevil Park can also be dangerous. Even if you do get to go on all the rides—and as often as you'd like—you may not be glad you did!

Good luck!

It's the third day you've been in bed with the flu, and you're getting pretty sick of just lying around watching television. You wish you could turn off the endless series of commercials unreeling before your eyes, but the remote is buried somewhere in the blankets at the foot of your bed, and you're too weak to get up. You roll over and close your eyes, wishing you could also close your ears, and block out the annoying sound.

You're about to drift off to sleep when the pounding rhythms of music unlike any you've ever heard catch your attention. The music sounds sinister, exciting, and scary all at the same time. You look back at the television just in time to see a series of images flash across the screen: a roller coaster zooms out of nowhere . . . a kayak plunges over a waterfall . . . a lion charges . . . a ghoulish face stares out a window of a spooky house.

"Daredevil Park—the most exciting place on Earth!" the announcer says.

You sit up straight. You can't believe it— Daredevil Park is finally going to open. It's supposed to be the greatest amusement park ever built! You and your friends had been hearing about it for years, but then rumors started to leak out that the rides were so dangerous the management couldn't risk letting anyone on them until they were made safer.

Turn to page 2.

The music ends, and a red devil wearing a crash helmet appears on the screen. His voice is even more sinister than the music: *"Daredevils, the park is opening exactly one month from today, but we're going to give four lucky winners a sneak preview! Yes, four lucky kids will get a thrill-packed, fun-filled weekend. They'll have the park all to themselves."*

You sit up even straighter. Imagine never having to wait on line to get on a ride! The last time you were at an amusement park, you spent most of the day standing in line. You remember spending two and a half hours waiting for ninety seconds of thrills on the roller coaster.

The TV daredevil picks up a phone. *"By the time I see you again, I'll have chosen at random the first four daredevils to experience the thrills and chills of Daredevil Park."* He holds the receiver toward you. *"If you want to be one of them, listen for my call, pick up the phone and say . . . 'I want to be a daredevil.'"*

You scramble around under the covers, looking for the remote. At last you find it under a comic book. You flick off the TV. You'll just have to miss watching the rest of the talk show about parties for pets; you'll need all your brain cells to concentrate on making the phone ring. You know it's a false hope—your chances of being selected are about one in a million—but false hope is all that you have. Daredevil Park is a thousand miles away, and the chances of your talking your parents into taking you there are about one in *two* million.

Go on to the next page.

With these thoughts zinging around in your brain, it's no wonder that when the phone rings it feels like an electric charge going through your body.

"I'll get it!" you scream, leaping out of bed. You feel dizzy and wobbly as you stagger down the hall toward the phone.

"You stay in bed!" your mother yells up to you in her most commanding voice.

You stop and wait for a wave of nausea to pass. You're about six feet away from the phone when it rings for the third time. You hear your mother's heels clicking across the kitchen, then stop as she picks up the receiver. You make a desperate lunge for the phone; your hands shake as you pick up the receiver and scream, "I want to be a daredevil!"

You recognize the voice of the TV daredevil as he says: *"Save your screams for the park, pal. You've won."*

"Won? Won what?" your mother says from the other phone in the kitchen.

Suddenly the chills, aches, and dizziness are too much for you. "I've got to get back in bed," you say. "Mom, be sure to get all the details and write down everything he says."

You grope your way down the hall back to your bed and climb in under the covers. You've won! As miserable as you are, there's a smile on your face as you drift off to sleep.

Turn to page 67.

The pickup is only inches from the back of the jeep when Walter, scared and confused, slams on his brakes. The truck plows into the jeep, causing it to spin around three times, then land on its side in the ditch next to the road.

Fortunately, everyone was wearing a seat belt, otherwise, you'd all have been killed. Except for a few cuts and bruises, everyone is okay. Walter seems a little dazed, and together you ease him out of the jeep and help him lie down in the grass.

"The car phone isn't working," Sam says after he gives it a try.

"Walter has a bad cut over his eye," says Leslie. "Let's see if we can find a first aid kit."

You're still shaking as you look over at the crumpled pickup truck a dozen feet away. The driver, a frail-looking man with shaggy gray hair, climbs out through the window.

For the moment you forget that you might be dealing with a dangerous nut. "Are you all right?" you ask, in a voice filled with concern.

The Bok brother ignores you and your question and instead peers over to where Leslie and Sam are applying a compress to Walter's wound. "Might have known it'd be Walter behind the wheel," he says in a grumpy voice. "Why they'd ever let you kids in a vehicle driven by him is beyond me. The way he just pokes along, he's dangerous."

Turn to page 62.

"They'll want to get some shots of you," Walter says, as the flashbulbs continue to pop.

You pose with several men in suits—big shots from the Daredevil Park organization, you suppose—then head off with Walter for the Daredevil Park Hotel.

The hotel is built to make you think you're still outside even though you're indoors. There's a waterfall cascading down a stone wall, and right next to it, a see-through elevator. You can tell that the hotel was just built—it smells like the inside of a new car.

"Pretty neat, huh?" says Walter as he picks up the key to your room.

"It is impressive," you say out loud. But I'm not here to hang around some hotel, you say to yourself. I'm here to ride the roller coaster.

Walter shows you to your room. "Dinner is at six. You'll meet the other three winners then," he tells you. "In the meantime, feel free to relax."

It's not so easy to relax. Now that you're finally here, you're all wound up, anxious to get started.

It's only an hour until dinner. In the meantime you could play with the Daredevil Park video games that are hooked up to the TV set in your room. You've heard the effects are awesome. Or you could explore the hotel—maybe even get an advance look at some of the rides.

If you choose to stay in your room until dinner, turn to page 108.

If you decide to explore the hotel, turn to page 14.

You check to make sure your door is unlocked. Then you grab the handle, yank it hard, and throw your shoulder against the door.

As you frantically try to open it, an image of Bok climbing through the window after the crash flashes through your mind. The door must have been damaged. It no longer opens from the inside!

"Hey, what do you think you're doing?" Bok says, reaching across and grabbing your arm.

You yank your arm away and pull yourself up through the window, but Bok grabs your leg and pulls you back in.

"Let me go!" you scream, kicking wildly.

Suddenly Bok lets go. But you're not out of the woods yet—and it looks like you never will be. One of your kicks has knocked Bok out, and his foot is pressing the accelerator down to the floorboard.

It wasn't such a good idea after all to try to escape from a moving vehicle driven by a madman, you think just before the pickup crashes into a mighty oak.

One thing's for sure: you'll never have a chance to make the same mistake again.

The End

You remember seeing a room service trolley in the hall just outside your room. It ought to do for a TV cart.

You open the door. Luck is with you; the trolley is still out there. Quickly you remove the remains of someone's lunch and wheel the trolley over to the television.

The makeshift cart is a lot wobblier than you'd like, but gradually you're able to ease the heavy set into place. You check to make sure the wires are clear of the wheels, then, holding the top-heavy set in place with one hand, you slowly move the set around to where you can see it from the bathtub.

Now for some fun!

You get out of your clothes, dim the lights, and turn on the great new game you've just discovered, Fourth of July Frenzy. Then you step into the whirlpool, through what has now become a mountain of bubbles, and stretch out in the water.

Perfect! You're so close to the television, it feels like you're right in the middle of the fireworks that are exploding from the screen—except you can't quite reach the joystick that controls the video games, you realize. All you have to do now is move the television set about nine inches closer.

Turn to page 69.

It's great to be treated like a hero, but it's not so great when you're told that Daredevil Park will have to be closed until all the rides are checked and retested.

Walter seems downcast as he settles next to you for the ride back home on the company jet. "Sometimes I think this place is jinxed," he says. "You, Leslie, and Sam may be the only three kids who will have ever experienced a Daredevil Park ride."

You certainly hope he's wrong, because you've all been invited to return when the park is finally ready to open. You'd hate to think this will be your last visit to what is really "the most exciting place on Earth—Daredevil Park!"

The End

Unfortunately, when you do this you also drag the towel over the delicately balanced television set, tipping it off its makeshift cart and into the bathtub.

Just before it hits the water, you watch the last exploding fireworks you'll ever see light up the television screen. A split second later, an electrical current surges through your body so fast you hardly have time to feel the pain.

The End

12

The scenery is entirely different on this side of the ravine—a grassy plain, punctuated by islands of rock. You're skirting one of these rocky areas when you hear something that makes you freeze in your tracks: a low, menacing growl.

The sound is coming from behind you. Slowly you turn your head, only to find that you're face-to-face with an enormous leopard crouched on a rocky ledge not twelve feet away from you. At least, you think it's a leopard. It could be just a very real-looking robot.

You might be standing in the Daredevil Park version of Africa, you try to reason. You remember hearing about something called the African Safari Adventure—one of those theme rides where you get to look at animals and have scary surprises as you're driven around in jeeps. But if that leopard is real, it looks like I'm in for the scariest adventure of my life, you think to yourself. You can't be sure, but your next move depends upon your gut feeling.

If you think the leopard is real, turn to page 81.

If you think it's a robot, turn to page 86.

14

You put your room key in your pocket and step out into the wide, carpeted hallway, ready to explore the hotel. As you head toward the elevator, you see a kid about your age emerge from the room next to yours.

"Aw, rats, I forgot my key!" he says, just as the door clicks shut behind him.

"You can get another one at the desk," you say.

"I guess I got sloppy," the boy says, shaking his head. "This is the first time since I left Dallas this morning that I've been without my guide. He's been taking care of everything."

You laugh. "I know what you mean. Mine is named Walter, but to tell you the truth, I'm glad to be without him for a while."

"I take it you're another winning daredevil?" he says, sticking out his hand. "My name's Tom Harber."

You introduce yourself as you shake his hand. "I was just going to go have a look around outside," you say.

Tom's eyes flash. "I had the same idea. I want to see some of the rides!"

The two of you take the glass elevator down to the lobby. Then you walk outside, cross a wide deck, and follow a winding path that leads to the entrance of the park.

Turn to page 70.

The vampire turns toward the bed and stealthily begins to move toward the sleeping girl.

It doesn't take a genius to figure out what he's about to do. Vampires are pretty reliable when it comes to their eating habits. You also predict that the girl will soon wake up and start screaming.

Even though the robots are amazingly lifelike, you're a little bored by the drama that you've seen played out at least a hundred times in movies and comic books. Instead you decide to have a look inside the coffin. There's no one around to stop you, and you'd love to know how the robots are controlled.

The vampire is about to sink his teeth into the girl's throat as you walk over to the coffin. Peering into the gloomy interior, you can just make out a small hinged panel on the bottom. There are probably some kind of electronic controls inside, you reason. You'd love to get your hands on them. Why, this is probably the only chance you'll ever have to control a vampire.

Turn to page 32.

"I'll just have a look around if it's all right with you, sir," you say evenly.

"Very well," Dr. Bok says. He reaches behind a rusty suit of armor and presses a button on the wall. An ancient-looking elevator descends, and Dr. Bok opens the creaky door, gesturing for you to step inside. "Better begin at the top. The lift will take you to the East Tower."

"Thanks," you say, as the door creaks shut behind you. You throw a smile at Dr. Bok, but it doesn't make the slightest dent in the stern expression on his face.

The elevator jerks upward a few feet, then stops. Then it continues to move shakily upward, accompanied by an alarming grinding sound. Being trapped in an elevator has never been one of your phobias, but you can't help but wonder whether this one is going to make it to the top. Your attention is diverted, however, by a strange whirring sound. It grows louder and louder as the elevator nears the top of the tower.

The elevator stops just as you figure out what must be making the sound. The thought makes you shudder. You put your arms over your face as the door opens only to find—

—Bats! Just as you thought, the whirring sound is coming from thousands of little bat wings, as they swoop and soar around the tower. Your skin crawls as they brush against your arms and legs. One of the little creatures gets caught in your hair. You scream and jump up and down, trying to untangle it.

Turn to page 72.

"Okay," you say to Tom, now taking the lead.

The two of you walk along the iron fence, looking for a way to get inside the park. It isn't long before you find what you're looking for.

A delivery van is parked alongside the fence. You look around to make sure nobody's watching, then climb up onto the hood of the van and from there onto the roof. Then it's just a jump, and a *thud*—and you're inside the park!

Tom lands beside you. You're a little shaken up, and Tom's rubbing his elbow, but he grins at you. "Hey, cool, we made it!" he says.

The two of you look around, then take a path that seems to be headed toward the roller coaster. At first you're both nervous about being spotted, but after a few minutes of scanning the scene warily, trying to make as little noise as possible, you decide it's okay to relax. The place seems to be completely deserted. There are no security guards around, no carpenters or computer experts making last-minute adjustments. There's nobody there except for you and Tom.

The path winds maddeningly past souvenir shops and fast-food restaurants. You don't seem to be making any headway.

"We're no closer to the roller coaster than we were when we started!" Tom complains after ten minutes of walking.

Turn to page 76.

You try to push the vampire out of the way, but robots, you discover with a sinking feeling, are much heavier than they look.

"Dr. Bok! Someone! Help!" you scream, but the organ music drowns out your frantic cries. You manage to flatten your body up against the side of the coffin so you won't be crushed, but there's no way you can prevent the lid from closing.

The organ music finally stops, and you yell as loud as you can, even though you know the chances of anyone hearing your muffled screams are practically zero. You manage to wriggle free of the robot's dead weight, but try as you might, you cannot lift the lid of the coffin.

There's no way to reach the control panel, and even if you could, you wouldn't be able to open it and push the buttons. Desperately you run your hands along the interior of the coffin, hoping to find a crack so that you'll have air to breathe. But as far as you can tell, your coffin is sealed as tightly as a tomb.

You lie down again, trying to use as little oxygen as possible, wondering how long you have before you're as lifeless as the vampire alongside you. Tears well up in your eyes. You pick up a corner of your companion's velvet cape and dab at your face.

Turn to page 75.

"Count me out," you say, shaking your head. "It's too risky."

"Okay, then . . . see you at dinner," Tom says.

You watch him walk along the fence, wishing you could have thought of a way to talk him out of entering the park. Then you head back to your room to put on your bathing suit.

Fifteen minutes later you've forgotten all about Tom. When you arrive at the pool, you find a boy and a girl floating around in inner tubes. They're probably the other two winning daredevils. You introduce yourself by doing a cannonball off the diving board.

The boy wipes the water you've splashed all over him out of his eyes and gives you a big grin. "Bet I get you back before the weekend's over," he says.

He gives you a watery handshake. "I'm Sam Brenner from Anchorage."

"You're from Alaska?" you say.

"I'm not from Anchorage, Florida," he replies.

The girl paddles up to you. "Hi, I'm Leslie Harris. Sam and I were wondering when we'd meet the other two winners. Have you met the other guy yet—Tom?"

You feel a stab of guilt. Tom could be in danger, wandering around Daredevil Park all by himself. But you don't want to be a tattletale. You're trying to figure out how to answer Leslie's question when suddenly a piercing alarm sounds, coming from inside the park.

Turn to page 40.

"I'm trying to see if I can get it going!" Tom says excitedly. "I've already got the power on. From the looks of it, it's all run by remote control once you get it started." He waves a small oblong item in your direction. "And here's the remote!"

Tom leaves the tower and climbs into the cage with you. He takes a place opposite you, then fastens his restraints.

"Tom! You're not actually going to—"

But you never get to finish your sentence. Tom pushes a button on the remote, and the cage begins to rise.

At first it rises slowly. Then it starts turning. Tom pushes a lever on the remote forward. The cage rises faster, then turns faster. Tom pushes the lever even farther. The cage turns faster—so fast you feel your body flattening out against the wall.

The cage reaches the top of the tower, then it plunges down. Tom looks at you with a fiendish smile as he pushes the lever all the way forward.

The cage spins faster and faster. You hear a whirring sound and watch as the bottom of the cage drops out from under your feet, and the top swings open over your head. You stare at the ground as you go plunging down. The cage stops just inches from impact, then shoots up again.

You look across the cage at Tom. Like you, he's plastered to the cage, his arms and legs stretched out along the sides. He has a look of terror on his face.

Turn to page 44.

You and Sam run down the stairs. "If you think I'm staying here all by myself, you're crazy!" Leslie says, following right behind you.

You follow the sounds of the skirmish to a small cabin. There you find the Indian grappling with a burly man in a Daredevil Park uniform.

"Stop!" you yell in the most commanding voice you can muster.

It almost works. The sound of authority in your voice causes the two men to freeze. They look at you for a second with startled faces, then go right back to fighting.

Sam grabs the Indian around the waist, and Leslie tackles him around the knees. You grab the Daredevil Park guy by the belt, but it's impossible to pry them apart. The three of you step back and watch helplessly, hoping that you're looking at a couple of actors playing out a scripted drama instead of a real struggle.

But something about the Indian tells you that he's no actor. He has the fiercest face you've ever seen. Bones pierce his ears and nose, and around his neck are necklaces of bone and teeth.

The Indian finally pins his burly opponent to the ground, then removes his belt and uses it to tie his hands behind his back. Then he turns his fierce-looking face toward you, Sam, and Leslie.

Turn to page 105.

Tom looks at you as he climbs into the back of the limousine. "Ride the big one an extra time for me," he says. He winks at you when he says this, but his voice sounds gruff, like he's trying to hold back tears.

You wave good-bye as you watch the limousine disappear. Then you head back to the hotel to change out of your bathing suit, wondering what other surprises your Daredevil Park weekend will bring.

A few minutes before six, you take the elevator down to the lobby. There you're greeted by your guide, Walter, looking a little ridiculous in a pith helmet and khaki shorts. He doesn't mention Tom by name, but he gives you a stern lecture about responsibility. It's a relief when he changes the subject and says, "We know you're anxious to get going on your first Daredevil Park ride, so to start off, we're having dinner on the Amazon River Boat."

"All right!" you say, as you follow Walter through the door of the hotel. A dune buggy is waiting for you there. Leslie and Sam are in the backseat. Walter gets in the driver's seat, and you hop in next to him up front.

Go on to the next page.

The dune buggy enters the park through a side gate, winds through a path for five minutes, then jerks to a stop. In front of you is a gleaming white boat about fifty feet long. The funny thing is, it seems to be floating in the air, on a thick cloud of fog.

"Where's the Amazon River?" you ask.

"You'll see," Walter says with a smile.

You follow Walter, Leslie, and Sam up a gangplank and onto the boat. The deck of the boat rolls gently under your feet, and you can hear the sound of water lapping against the hull.

"This is weird," Sam says to you in a whisper. "It really does feel like we're on water."

Turn to page 100.

You stare at the sights in front of your eyes, unable to say a word. Your boat, you now see, is on a mighty river winding through a thick tropical jungle. Trees that look to be a hundred feet tall line the riverbank; vines wrap themselves around tree trunks and dangle from branches; a flock of brilliantly colored birds flies overhead; masses of butterflies appear out of nowhere, and as quickly disappear.

"A jungle? I don't remember seeing this from the airplane when I flew in today," says Leslie.

"It looks real," you say, "but it's probably all an illusion. They say Daredevil Park has the most advanced special effects of any amusement park ever built. I read that the animatronics are ten times more sophisticated than the ones at Disneyland."

"Animatronics? What are those?" Sam asks.

Just then a flock of monkeys swing by, feeding on leaves and chattering amongst themselves. One of them has a baby wrapped tightly around her middle.

"Computer-animated people, animals—like those monkeys," you say. "The neat thing is, they mix the robotics up with real animals, so you never quite know whether what you're looking at is real or a robot."

Just then Leslie clutches your arm. "Is *he* for real?" she asks, pointing off into the distance.

You look upriver. A rough wooden canoe, paddled by a fierce-looking fellow, is heading toward you.

Turn to page 90.

As you reach the loading block, you look over your shoulder at Sam and Leslie. They're both white-faced.

"Awesome," Sam whispers.

But what's this? Instead of remaining at the loading dock, you bypass it as the roller coaster cars are shuttled onto some kind of turntable. The cars rotate, then they start making the initial climb all over again, except this time you're riding backward—you're about to experience the Black Hole's "alternate universe!"

Going backward is even more stomach-churning and mind-boggling than your frontward ride was. By the time you've looped the last loop and screamed around the last hairpin curve, you're so disoriented you wonder if you'll even be able to stand up again.

Sure enough, when the roller coaster attendant helps you out of your seat, you stagger around with your friends for a good ten minutes, laughing hysterically, before you feel even halfway back to normal.

As soon as your stomach stops flip-flopping and you can get your eyes to focus, the three of you get back into the jeep with Walter.

"Where to now?" he asks.

By now you and your two friends are able to read each other's minds. You look at each other, then say together: "Downhill Racer!"

"Downhill Racer it is," Walter says, and you're on your way.

Turn to page 60.

Dr. Bok pushes another button and a second television monitor comes to life. This one shows a skeleton running through another room in the mansion.

"Look at the way that skeleton moves!" Dr. Bok says. "I worked twenty-two years perfecting the animatronics that bring life to all these ghastly, wonderful creatures." You're alarmed to see that this mad scientist is working himself up, getting more and more agitated.

Crazily, he skitters around the room from computer to computer, flicking buttons, turning on several more television monitors which show other rooms in the mansion. "All this for *what?*" he says. "So I could be fired from my job just six days before Daredevil Park is scheduled to open!"

Dr. Bok puts his face up next to yours. His left eyebrow twitches wildly, and a vein stands out on his forehead.

You rock your chair in an effort to put some distance between you and the doctor.

"Why?" he says, then pauses, trembling with rage. "Because they say my beautiful effects, my brilliant animatronics, my fabulous rides are *too dangerous!*"

Abruptly, he turns around and slumps in a chair behind the desk next to you. "What can I do?" he says in a small, defeated voice.

Turn to page 92.

30

Music—a happy waltz—begins. Then the merry-go-round starts to spin, picking up speed. You turn the lever Dr. Bok showed you and adjust it so it's going just fast enough to keep him from escaping.

You don't have long to wait before almost a dozen cop cars pull up. A young police officer dashes over to where you're standing.

"He's all yours, officer," you say, gesturing toward the whirling merry-go-round.

The police officer pushes his hat back on his head and looks with amazement from you to the whirling Bok. "I don't know exactly what you did, but I know it took guts," he says.

Turn to page 10.

"We'll find out soon enough," you say, as you hear a motorboat pulling alongside your vessel.

Several security guards and an expensively dressed executive climb on board.

"Take him!" the executive orders as they burst into the cabin.

"Not unless you take us, too!" you say. The three of you quickly form a protective wall between Kayano and the guards.

The guards look at you, stunned, then at the executive, wondering what to do.

Leslie glares at the executive, a gray-haired man with steady blue eyes. "This so-called Amazon Adventure portrays Indians as a bunch of wild men who attack innocent people," she says hotly.

Kayano's face relaxes, and he gives a little snort of recognition when he hears Leslie repeating what he has just said, almost word for word.

The executive remains calm. "I'm Bernard Weston, president of the Daredevil Park Corporation," he says, extending his hand to Kayano. "Now I suggest we all sit down and talk things over. If there's something offensive in our Amazon drama, I want to know about it."

This guy didn't get to the top for no reason, you think to yourself as you watch Mr. Weston skillfully question Kayano. In less than fifteen minutes he's agreed to close the Amazon Adventure until the script can be rewritten. He's even hired Kayano to help rewrite it!

Turn to page 74.

32

Because the coffin is much deeper than you thought it would be, you can't quite reach the controls from where you're standing. You climb inside, and sure enough, when you open the panel, you find a dozen switches, dials, and buttons. If only you had a flashlight, you could get a better look at them.

The girl's screams have been replaced by gloomy organ music, and you hear the mechanical sound of footsteps approaching. You look up to see the vampire returning to his coffin. You start to stand up, but his leg hits you on the side of the head and knocks you down.

"Hey, watch what you're doing!" you say. But of course robots can't watch what they're doing. They can only do what they're programmed to do, and this one is programmed to climb back into his coffin and slam the lid.

Turn to page 19.

You decide to stay back with Leslie. "Be careful!" you say to Sam as he starts down the stairs.

Leslie puts her hands over her ears and runs to the far end of the ship's deck, trying to get as far away from the fighting as she can.

"There's probably nothing to worry about," you say once you've reached her side, trying to reassure yourself as much as Leslie.

She looks down at the water, then over toward the jungle. "It's only about twenty-five feet down to the water," she says. "And the land can't be more than about a hundred feet away."

You can tell what her next suggestion is going to be. And with Sam's shouts now joining the other angry voices, you're anxious to get as far away as you can, too. "Let's go for it," you say quickly.

Together you climb up onto the rail; then you jump.

Too bad you didn't think your decision through. Some of Daredevil Park is real, as you know, and some of it is just an illusion. Unfortunately, the water on this side of the ship is no more than a shimmering effect. Instead of splashing down, you *smash* down—onto unyielding cement. Maybe one person in a thousand could survive such a brutal fall. But you and Leslie aren't going to beat the odds.

The End

An hour later, the president of Daredevil Park is listening to your account of what happened on Transylvania Island.

"He really planned to dynamite the mansion," he says, shaking his head in disbelief. He picks up a phone. "I want every ride, every fast-food outlet, and every corner of this place checked by security. Daredevil Park is closed until further notice."

As you return home, you wonder if you will be invited back because of your heroic work uncovering the evil Dr. Bok's scheme, or if you will be banned from Daredevil Park because of all the rules you had to break in order to do it?

Only time will tell.

The End

The path to the roller coaster takes you past one of the strangest-looking rides you've ever seen: it consists of a hundred-foot tower and a dozen or so round cages mounted on steel arms that stick out in every direction. Some of the cages are high in the air. Others are closer to the ground. Each cage is equipped with restraints for four people.

Tom reads the huge sign on top of the tower: THE WHIRLING DERVISH. "How do you think it works?" he asks, as the two of you examine one of the cages.

"I don't know," you say, climbing up into the cage. You stick your arms through the restraints. "I suppose you stand against the side of the cage like this, and these straps keep you from bouncing around inside."

You fiddle with the restraints until you have them fastened across your chest. Then you feel a tiny lurch as the cage moves forward a couple of inches. You crane your neck around, looking for Tom. He's inside the tower. Through an open door at the base you see him standing in front of some kind of electronic control panel.

"Tom, what are you doing?" you say sharply.

Turn to page 21.

You're surprised to find that you feel no pain, just fear. Next comes the gentle sensation of flying through the air, and finally, a shuddering jolt as your kayak hits the water so hard that it seems to plunge twenty feet under, then rise to the surface in agonizingly slow motion.

You look around, stunned, as your kayak proceeds slowly to the unloading dock. You watch Leslie, then Sam splash down behind you. They have the same look of shock on their faces as you do.

Once it hits you that you're still alive, you break out into hysterical laughter. "We made it!" you yell to Leslie and Sam.

"That was the wildest ride of my life!" Sam yells back.

As you reach the unloading dock, Mr. Weston himself is waiting for you with his most genial executive smile. He sticks his hand out to help you up from your kayak.

"Mr. Weston, you've got a real hit," you tell him, catching your balance. You look down at your arms and legs. Something seems wrong. It suddenly dawns on you. "I thought I was going to drown a couple of times—but I'm not even the slightest bit wet!"

Go on to the next page.

"It's the work of our state-of-the-art special effects," he tells you. "So much happens on that ride so fast, you *think* you're going through torrents of water, when actually you're not."

Leslie looks at her watch as she climbs out of her kayak. "I can't believe it. The ride only lasted seven minutes from dock to dock. It seemed a lot longer."

Mr. Weston nods thoughtfully. "When your mind and body are bombarded with new sensations, time seems to stretch." He puts a hand on your shoulder. "I'm glad you kids like what you've seen of this place. But you'd better get some rest now. We've got a big day planned for you tomorrow."

Back in your hotel, you put on your pajamas and climb into bed. You intend to watch a little television before you go to sleep, but you're so tired, you feel as if you really *did* spend hours racing rapids. In a few short minutes, you're asleep.

Turn to page 84.

You see a security guard rushing toward the big gate that marks the entrance. He's reaching for his walkie-talkie with one hand and his pistol with the other!

You pull yourself up over the side of the pool and run toward the gate. Several more security guards converge there as you arrive on the scene, just in time to see a dune buggy lurch by, going much too fast. With a sinking feeling you realize that Tom is behind the wheel, and more than likely he doesn't know the first thing about driving.

The dune buggy crashes through a split-rail fence, then knocks over a hot dog cart, climbs over a low stone wall, and splashes down into a pond.

Turn to page 53.

The voice sends shivers down your spine, making the hair stand up on the back of your neck. You step back and remind yourself that this isn't real, that it is only an amusement park. But it doesn't seem to help. Added to your fears is the uneasy knowledge that you're not even supposed to be here in the first place.

You almost hope the door will be locked up tight, but as you grasp one of the huge door handles and pull, you can feel it start to open. Fiendish laughter comes from inside. Somehow it's even creepier than the moaning voice.

You could turn back. No one would ever have to know you were too scared to go inside all by yourself. Still, you've come this far. It would be a shame not to go through with it.

If you decide to turn back, turn to page 64.

If you choose to go inside, turn to page 47.

Fifteen minutes later, you're peering nervously down the twists and turns of a white-water river running through a rocky canyon. In front of you is a waterfall that plummets fifty feet into a whirlpool. From there, the water continues its mad descent down the canyon.

You've been elected to go first. Mr. Weston himself helps you adjust your safety helmet. "It's equiped with a CB radio," he tells you. "To help you through the course, Vince here will be talking you down." He nods toward a technician wearing earphones.

You give the strap on your helmet a final tug, then look over your shoulder to where Sam and Leslie are seated, ready to follow behind you. You're already strapped into the Daredevil Park version of a kayak—a small craft just big enough for one person. You grip the paddle tightly, ready to row like crazy to keep yourself from being hurled against the huge boulders and the rocky face of the canyon—even though you know that this is an amusement park ride, and the paddle won't do you any good.

"Good luck," says Mr. Weston, as you feel your kayak start to move over the edge of the waterfall. "You're the first kids to ever experience White Water Rapids, and you won't be the last. Our research shows it's destined to be one of Daredevil Park's most popular rides."

Turn to page 82.

44

You're pinned so tightly against the sides of the cage that you don't even need your restraints, you think to yourself. You're being held in place by the centrifugal force generated by the whirling cage.

It's the most thrilling ride you've ever experienced. You close your eyes and let yourself enjoy the strange, wonderful, frightening sensations that have taken over your body. You try to give Tom the thumbs-up sign to let him know you're having a fantastic time, but it requires too much effort to move your thumb. You wonder if you can even open your eyes anymore at this point.

It's not easy, but when you finally do get them open, you feel sick at what you see—the remote has gotten away from Tom. It's plastered to the side of the cage a good six inches away from his outstretched hand. You're destined to go on spinning around and around until someone comes to rescue you—and it could take a long time for that to happen, you realize.

If only you could get your hands on the remote. You stare at it, wishing it would slide close enough for you to grab it. But you realize it's not going to move. It's practically glued to its spot.

Turn to page 58.

46

There's nothing you can do but watch helplessly as the huge boulder careens toward you. Your boat is moving at a maddeningly slow rate on this flat stretch of water. You paddle like a maniac, trying to get out of the way. You've never been so scared in all your life.

Nothing could prepare you for the enormous splash as the boulder plunges into the water not three feet from your kayak! The sound is deafening. The boat rocks crazily, and water pours over you, but at least you weren't crushed to death. Only then do you remember that you're in an amusement park. There's no way you could have been hurt—at least that's what you hope. Right now you just want to concentrate on getting through the next few minutes alive.

"It can't get any scarier," you say out loud, hoping it will give you courage.

"Oh yes, it can," says Vince. You grip your paddle tightly as you hear the noise of churning water up ahead, then you gasp as you round a bend in the stream and see the rock-strewn rapids dropping off before you.

The granite walls of the canyon are so narrow here, and the drop-off so steep, that the river is transformed into the raging white water that gives this ride its name.

Turn to page 93.

Your heart races wildly as you step through the front door, into the dark interior of the mansion. Once your eyes get accustomed to the gloom, you see that you're in a forbiddingly dingy hall. A huge stone staircase is in front of you. Over your head is a massive chandelier. Gloomy faces—portraits in crooked, ornate frames—stare down at you from the walls. Hung over the portraits are enough old swords and shields to outfit at least fifty knights. A suit of armor stands in one corner. Everything is covered with thick dust and cobwebs. The only movement in the room is the pendulum of a huge grandfather clock; the only sound its ponderous ticking.

Cautiously you enter the enormous room that lies beyond the entrance hall. It is as still and as quiet as a tomb. You try not to make any sounds and break the gloomy silence.

Suddenly you feel a heavy hand clamping down on your shoulder. You gasp and whirl around to find yourself looking into the face of a man with piercing black eyes and wiry gray hair. His scowling mouth is partly obscured by a thick mustache.

"I thought I told you to stay away," he says, with frightening intensity. He scans your face. What he sees only seems to make him scowl harder. "A child! A very *daring* child—or perhaps a foolhardy one."

Turn to page 104.

The haunted mansion is so realistic, you'd half-expected to be led down into a dank and dreary dungeon. But instead you find yourself in a squeaky-clean, brightly lit room filled with electronic equipment and television monitors. They're all hooked into a central computer, you notice, which in turn is hooked into several satellite computers.

Dr. Bok points to a chair near the central computer. "Sit," he says. Then he goes to a closet and starts rummaging around for something. "I am glad to have a visitor. It's always fun to show someone intelligent the way things work."

He rummages around some more. "Ah, found it," he says.

As he walks back over to where you're sitting, the doctor holds something behind his back. He forces what looks like the first smile he's ever smiled onto his sickly yellow face.

Something about this guy gives you the creeps. Maybe you should get out of here. It should be fairly easy to beat it back up the stairs. On the other hand, he's probably just a harmless eccentric— you'd rather not give up your behind-the-scenes look at Daredevil Park if you don't have to.

If you decide to make a run for it, turn to page 87.

If you choose to stay, turn to page 98.

Dr. Bok examines the dynamite in his hand. You feel a tiny surge of hope. Maybe you can talk him out of his idea, you think. "With all due respect, sir, it's wrong to deprive kids of the Transylvania Island experience. And even though they changed your ideas a little bit, you're still the genius behind the whole thing."

Dr. Bok fingers the dynamite thoughtfully.

"When people find out who the real inventor of Daredevil Park is, I'll bet the press will be all over you for interviews," you continue. "You'll probably even be asked to be on the big talk shows. I'll bet someone will even want to sign you to a book contract." You're really rolling now, you say to yourself. "They might even make a movie about you!"

Dr. Bok puts the dynamite down on the desk and looks at you earnestly. "Do you really think so?" he asks.

You give him your friendliest smile. "Hey, I just had a neat idea!" you say. "Why don't we call a press conference. Then the newspapers and television reporters will have the real story about who's responsible for this fabulous place! I'll help you set it up."

Go on to the next page.

Dr. Bok runs his hand through his wiry gray hair. "I thought of going to the press . . ." he begins, but lets his sentence trail off.

"If you'll just be kind enough to undo some of these knots," you say, "I could get the use of my hands back and start phoning around for you. When the press hears you have something to say to them, I'll bet they'll come right over."

Turn to page 96.

You feel pretty foolish as you look toward the leopard and shake your head. "I guess you think it was pretty stupid of me to stand here all night," you say.

The driver, a young man wearing a "Save the Whales" T-shirt, looks at you solemnly. "Not at all. We wouldn't be doing our job if we couldn't fool people into thinking our robots were real."

He helps you into the cab of the truck, then climbs into the driver's seat next to you and picks up a phone. "Ed Jackson here," he says. "I've found the missing daredevil." He talks a few minutes, then hangs up. "Looks like you're going to be sent home," he says, patting you on the shoulder. "You've already caused more than your share of trouble."

You sigh, discouraged, as you think of all the fun you could have had. If only you hadn't tried to be such a daredevil!

The End

By the time you scramble over the stone wall, the dune buggy has sunk, and Tom is treading water.

"Tom!" you yell.

He looks at you, a stunned expression on his face. Then he smiles weakly. "I decided to go for a swim after all," he says.

You jump in the water after him. With a couple of strokes you reach his side. "Are you all right?" you ask.

"I'm okay," he says. "But that dune buggy down there might not have much of a future."

A security guard joins the two of you in the water. "Take it easy, son. We'll have you out in just a second," he says to Tom in a soothing tone. But later, when everyone learns that Tom is unhurt, the tone isn't so soothing.

"In just five minutes you've ruined fifty thousand dollars' worth of Daredevil Park," Tom's guide tells him as he escorts him into a limousine. "It's back to Dallas for you before you do any more damage."

Turn to page 24.

54

"See you later," you say to Tom, as you start down the path to Transylvania Island. You can't help but wonder if you'll ever get to see your reckless companion again.

Soon you leave the food stands and souvenir shops behind and enter a desolate area. As you move through dense woods—actually dead trees covered with dangling strands of moss—the path narrows.

You walk along the winding path until you reach a wooden bridge that stretches over a stagnant green swamp. The bridge then disappears into a low, thick, greenish-gray fog. Nailed to a post is a large sign that reads ENTER AT YOUR OWN RISK.

Excitement fills you as you realize that you've reached the entrance to Transylvania Island. You step onto the bridge and disappear into the greenish fog.

You grope your way across the bridge, holding on to a rough wooden guardrail, only to jump back in horror as you find that you're touching a human skull! By the time you get to the other side of the bridge, the fog has thinned out just enough for you to make out the silhouette of a huge, dark mansion ahead of you.

Turn to page 88.

Thanks to a stiff current, you're moving away from the treacherous Dr. Bok. At least you've escaped, you think.

As you float along, you rehearse what you'll be saying to the press about your adventures on Transylvania Island.

But you never do get to meet the press. Minutes later, you hear the pounding roar of falling water. Seconds after that, you're going over a waterfall. It would be a thrilling sensation if it were an amusement park ride. But unfortunately, it's not.

The End

58

Suddenly an idea hits you. Since you don't need your restraints to hold you in the cage, maybe you could get out of them and ease your way over to where the remote is. It's a long shot, but you don't think you can take much more of this ride. Still, it might be safer to just wait for someone to rescue you.

If you try to get the remote, turn to page 112.

If you choose to wait for someone to rescue you, turn to page 80.

"This is Dr. Bok," he says into a hand mike attached to the computer. "I am glad you are here. If you will go through the door on your left"—he pushes a lever on the computer—"which is now opening, you will find a staircase leading down to the control room, where we will conduct the interview."

Dr. Bok looks toward you for approval.

"Very clever, doctor," you say.

You hear footsteps on the staircase, and soon a young woman appears, followed by a man carrying a videocam and another man with some lighting equipment.

"I'm Jeanette Wallace, from Channel Five News at Six," the young woman says. She looks around the large room. "Let's get you set up over here in front of the television monitors," she says briskly, leading Dr. Bok across the room.

You try to think of a way to signal one of them to call the police, but everything's happening too fast. The camera crew is busy with their equipment, and Miss Wallace is doing her professional best to get Dr. Bok relaxed before the camera. You decide it would be better to just let them go ahead with the interview while you try to think of what to do.

Turn to page 95.

You're relaxing in the backseat of Walter's jeep, enjoying the passing scene, when he suddenly swerves off the road, avoiding a collision with a truck. "Yikes!" Leslie says, "Someone ought to teach that guy how to drive."

Walter's face has turned white. "Uh-oh, this could mean trouble," he says.

Quickly, he changes course, driving the jeep down another dirt path, away from your destination. He grabs the cellular phone in the jeep. "This is Walter. I just spotted one of the Bok brothers heading south on Daredevil Drive. He passed me just outside the Nervous Elephant, doing about sixty." You recognize the name of the restaurant you just passed. Walter looks grim as he hangs up the phone. "That was one of the Bok brothers," he informs you.

"Who are the Bok brothers?" Sam asks.

"They're the geniuses who invented Daredevil Park," Walter says, with a sweeping gesture meant to take in everything. "Twins—engineers with a fantastic inventive knack for creating special effects."

"So outside of being a terrible driver, what's wrong with the guy?" asks Leslie.

"Perhaps nothing," says Walter. "You see, they're both terrible drivers, but only one of them is a terrible person. Since they're identical twins, I'm not sure which twin nearly ran us off the road."

Turn to page 97.

The Bok brother reaches up and forces open the damaged door on the passenger side of his truck, then gestures for you to get in. "Well, come on," he says. "I need some help if I'm going to get this place ready in time for opening day!"

You're so flabbergasted by this guy's behavior, you just stand there staring at him. To your horror, he reaches into his belt and pulls out a gun. "If you're not going to come voluntarily, perhaps this will persuade you," he says.

You have no choice but to get into the truck. The engine is still running you notice. Bok climbs into the driver's seat, puts the truck in gear, and slams his foot down on the accelerator. As you roar past your friends, they look up with shocked expressions, surprised to see the pickup careening down the road with you inside.

All you can do now is manage to stay in your seat as the Bok brother swerves off the road, taking off across a bumpy field. No ride at Daredevil Park could provide the kind of bone-rattling experience that you're getting right now.

As you lurch across to the other side of the field, the pickup turns onto a scarred path and into a wooded area. Here the ruts are so deep that your driver is forced to slow down. You brace yourself against the dashboard to keep from being thrown against the ceiling of the cab.

Go on to the next page.

Your kidnapper is concentrating so hard on his driving, he seems to have forgotten all about you. Now that he's slowed down, you could try to jump out and escape through the woods.

However, you could get hurt pretty badly leaping from a moving truck. And since you're riding through thick woods, there's always the danger you'll jump straight into a tree. Whatever your decision, you'll have to make it fast.

---

*If you decide to jump out of the truck,
turn to page 7.*

If you decide it's too risky, turn to page 109.

I'm getting away from this creepy place, you think, as you run back down the path and back onto the bridge.

The green fog is as thick as ever, and you have to slow down as you grope your way across the bridge. But your mind doesn't slow down. In fact, terrifying thoughts continue to race through your head. You're so panicky you don't even bother to look for a path through the woods. It isn't long before you realize that you're lost.

Somehow you can't get yourself to calm down. Instead, you just keep running on and on. You feel the branches of the trees tearing at your clothes. By the time you make it through the woods, you're a sweaty, panting mess.

Safely out of the forest, you see the towers of the Daredevil Park Hotel off on the horizon. You sigh with relief and head toward them.

You haven't gotten very far before you come to a stone wall. It's easy to climb up the wall, but on the other side, you realize, is a thirty-foot-deep ravine. Both the wall and the ravine run as far as your eye can see in either direction.

Carefully, you make your way down the wall to the bottom of the ravine, then scramble up the other side. You stop to brush the dirt off yourself, then continue on toward the hotel. You notice that the sun is low on the horizon—if you don't hurry, you won't make it back before dark.

Turn to page 12.

You step into the road and wave your arms, signaling the driver to stop. The jeep moves steadily, continuing toward you. When it's about thirty feet away, you realize that it isn't slowing down. It's too inconceivable, and you don't even try to get out of the way. Surely it's going to stop!

But it doesn't. Just before you feel the hard metal plow into your body, you catch a quick look at the driver. His smile seems a little too mechanical. You weren't fooled by the leopard, and this guy doesn't fool you any, either. However, knowing that he's a robot doesn't do you the least bit of good now.

The End

Exactly one month later you catch your first glimpse of Daredevil Park as the private jet you're on comes in for a landing. Swooping down through the clouds that have been obscuring your view, you register the sight of lots of water and the twists and spirals of a huge roller coaster.

"That's our roller coaster," says the young man beside you unnecessarily. His name is Walter, and he's from Daredevil Park's public relations department—your official guide. You'd kind of hoped to make the trip without any grownups along, but putting up with Walter is better than having your parents around. "It's called the Black Hole, and it's the largest roller coaster in the world," Walter says proudly.

The poor guy is doing everything he can to make you like him. You just wish he didn't talk like a sales brochure all the time. You nod politely as the small aircraft skids to a stop.

"Well, here we are!" Walter says, as if you couldn't tell that for yourself.

You unbuckle your seat belt and climb out onto the tarmac. Fifty feet away you see a limousine waiting for you. It'll be your second limousine ride of the day.

A bunch of reporters are standing in a huddle nearby. As you near the limousine, several of them point their cameras at you and start flashing away.

Turn to page 6.

Minutes later you enter Kiddeeland, a part of the park where everything is scaled down in size and excitement. Dr. Bok skirts the edge of a ride that features little pink elephants and pulls into a garage.

"Don't try any funny stuff," Dr. Bok says menacingly, as he pats the gun in his belt.

"Funny stuff" is exactly what you're waiting for the opportunity to try, but instead you nod meekly, get out of the truck as you're told to, and help the doctor hide it under a big tarp.

Bok then leads you to the fanciest merry-go-round you've ever seen. You would have loved it when you were about five years old.

Dr. Bok opens the door to a little booth next to the merry-go-round and motions for you to follow him inside. "These are the controls that run this thing," he says, pointing to a metal panel with several levers and dials. "It's pretty simple to operate." He points to a switch. "That turns it on." He touches a lever. "And this controls the speed."

Dr. Bok reaches into his pocket for a screwdriver, then removes the cover of the panel, revealing a tangle of wires. "I'm going to make sure that anybody who climbs on one of those horses gets a very special surprise."

Dr. Bok studies the wires, then settles down for some serious tinkering.

Turn to page 111.

You get to your feet carefully; the bottom of the bathtub is very slippery from all the shampoo you poured into the water.

You know better than to touch an electrical appliance while you're wet, so you reach for a towel from the rack just next to the television before you start to climb out of the tub.

Like everything else in the Daredevil Park Hotel, the towel is extra-big. You have to really yank at it to pull it off the rack. As you do, you feel your feet starting to slide out from under you. There's no way you're going to keep your balance.

Splash! You fall back into the tub. You come up coughing, and instinctively you take the end of the towel and put it to your face in order to wipe away the bubbles.

Turn to page 11.

70

The enormous entrance is locked up tight. A huge, glittery sign across the top of the iron gate reads GRAND OPENING! A much smaller sign on the fence reads NO TRESPASSING.

"Looks like we aren't going to get to see anything until tomorrow," you say. "Let's check out the pool and go for a swim instead."

"We shouldn't give up so fast," Tom says. "I'll bet if we follow the fence, we'll find a way to get inside."

"But the sign," you say, feeling uncomfortable. "We'd be trespassing."

"Nobody'd have to know," Tom says. "Besides, think of the fun we'd have without our guides watching every move we make. We have plenty of time—we'll be back before dinner, and no one will even know we've left the hotel."

It would be fun, you think. And Tom seems so sure of himself. But a swim would be nice, too; certainly less risky.

If you decide to try to get inside the park with Tom, turn to page 18.

If you choose to go for a swim instead, turn to page 20.

They're only robot bats, you keep telling yourself, as you stumble across the tower. But they definitely look like the real thing. They even have a sharp, musty smell, just as you'd expect from a bat.

You reach the narrow stone staircase on the other side of the room. The bats aren't programmed to follow you down the stairs, you soon see, but you keep your head down and your hands in front of your face nonetheless.

By the time you reach the bottom of the stairs, you must be two or three levels below the bat tower, you figure. You're still a little shaky as you enter a large chamber.

Most of the room is dimly lit by moonlight streaming in through an open window, but a shaft of light draws your attention to a huge four-poster bed where a beautiful, golden-haired girl lies sleeping.

The only movement in the room is the rise and fall of her chest; the only sound her even breathing.

Go on to the next page.

Everything is peaceful and calm, and yet you feel your body tense, waiting for some drama to unfold.

You don't have to wait long. The sound of creaking hinges draws your eyes to a large oblong box in the far corner of the room—a coffin. The top of the box is slowly being pushed open from the inside by a man's arm. Soon he emerges from the coffin. He's a tall, thin man with a very pale face. As he adjusts his black and red cape over his black suit, he seems to be staring straight at you. Then he opens his mouth in a horrible smile, exposing two fanglike teeth. You're looking into the eyes of a vampire!

Turn to page 15.

Everyone gets in the motorboat for a ride back to land. By the time you dock, Mr. Weston has arranged to have Kayano flown back to the University of New Mexico on the company jet. Then he turns his steady blue eyes on you and your friends. "Instead of going back to the hotel, how would you like to ride the White Rapids?" he asks.

The White Rapids! "Sounds good to me," you say, remembering the awesome sight of a kayak plunging over a waterfall in the Daredevil Park television commercial.

Both Sam and Leslie have that scared, eager look on their faces that tells you they're more than willing to join you.

Turn to page 43.

You don't know how long it is that you lie there, terrified, in the pitch dark. But after what could be either twenty minutes or twenty hours, you hear the sweetest sound you've ever heard in your life: the gloomy organ music that announces the beginning of the vampire drama.

You feel the vampire next to you come to life, and soon you see light as he opens the lid of the coffin. As soon as he's halfway out, you leap to your feet.

"I'm alive! I'm alive!" you shout as the vampire makes his way over to the girl.

She starts screaming, but then everything stops. A Daredevil Park executive steps forward. "Are you all right?" he asks.

"Just a little stiff," you say, moving your arms and legs.

The executive looks at you coldly. "You'd be a lot stiffer if we found you much later."

"How long was I trapped?" you ask.

"Who knows? We do know that you disappeared eight hours ago and every person on our staff has been looking for you since then," he says, leading you away. "It's a good thing for you we have this place covered with video cameras."

The management wastes no time putting you on the company jet and sending you back home. It's too bad—those hours inside the coffin will probably be the only hours you ever spend at Daredevil Park.

The End

You round a bend and come upon a fork in the road where the path splits. There's a sign that reads:

"The Black Hole is to the left. Come on!" says Tom.

"Maybe we should go right," you say. "Transylvania Island is supposed to be really spooky. And since you walk through it, there's a better chance we'd actually get to see something."

"You don't think we're going to the roller coaster just to look at it do you?" Tom says. He points off in the distance, where you can make out a string of roller coaster cars inching their way up to its highest point. "It's rolling, and we could be the first kids in the whole world to ride it!"

"But whoever's testing it right now will spot us," you say.

"We won't know that unless we try," says Tom. He gives you a nudge. "Hey, we got this far, didn't we?"

Tom certainly is a daredevil. You *would* like to be the first, but it won't be as easy to sneak onto a roller coaster as it was to sneak into the park. Besides, you're very curious about Transylvania Island.

If you choose to go with Tom to the Black Hole, turn to page 37.

If you decide to visit Transylvania Island instead, turn to page 54.

Bump after bump after bump, you can feel your whole body shaking with the shock. Then, up ahead, you see a smooth expanse of snow, and beyond it, nothing but air.

You gasp, trying to stay on the trail, but the magnetic remote that controlls your body has other ideas. You can feel yourself being hurled into space, your body leaning forward.

As you soar through the air, time seems suspended. Surprisingly, you make a perfect landing, then continue to ski on down the trail.

Now you're threading your way through the poles of a racecourse. You detect crowds lining the sides, shouting and whistling, encouraging you on your way down the mountain. Up ahead, a banner is stretched over the finish line, marking the end of the race.

The poles marking the slalom portion of the course are behind you now. Nothing stands between you and the finish line except a final icy slope so steep it's practically vertical. Your body crouches in a tucked position, and you scream as you head straight down the mountain.

The crowd roars as you cross the finish line. A sign informs you that you've been clocked at ninety miles per hour. You straighten up, a big grin on your face, and raise your arms in triumph as you glide to a halt near a race official.

Turn to page 101.

"I'll come with you," you say to Dr. Bok. "I'd rather see how all these audio-animatronics work."

Dr. Bok's left eyebrow twitches. "Ah, so you're able to throw around big words, like audio-animatronics! Most kids your age don't know what to call objects that are animated electronically. Perhaps you *will* understand what I am about."

The doctor opens a rusty iron door. Beyond it you can see a staircase leading down. "This way," he says, and you follow him down the stairs.

Turn to page 49.

Getting out of your restraints doesn't seem like such a smart thing to do, you decide. Instead, you try to relax while you're waiting to be rescued, but already you're starting to feel sick. Is it possible to spin to death?

Ten hours later you learn the answer to your question when someone finally realizes that the Whirling Dervish is still running, even though the engineer everyone thought was giving it a final test has gone home hours before.

By the time a Daredevil Park security guard peels you and Tom from the sides of your cage, it feels like you've turned to jelly. You can't stand up, let alone walk, and the world, it seems, will never stop spinning.

An overnight stay in the hospital gets you back to normal. As your disappointed guide escorts you onto a plane to take you back home, you wonder if you'll ever get to see the inside of Daredevil Park again—or if you even want to.

The End

The leopard looks like he could pounce on you at any minute, you think, feeling a chill run down your spine.

You don't want to do anything to threaten him, so you just stand there, trying to remain absolutely still.

Hours go by. You hear the leopard growl from time to time; you dare not make a move.

You watch the sun go down and the stars come out. You can see the lights twinkle on in the Daredevil Park Hotel, but the only sign of life for miles around is the figure of the menacing leopard right before you.

Maybe it's sheer terror that gives you your strength, but somehow you manage to keep standing there all night long.

Shortly after dawn, you watch as a big truck drives across the grass. It pulls up near you, and the driver looks from you to the leopard, then back to you again. He gets out of his jeep and calmly walks over to where you're standing.

"Don't worry, kid, he's not going to attack," the driver says. "This leopard here's a robot."

Relieved, you collapse in a heap. Tears sting your eyes as you feel sharp pains shoot through your legs—the result of standing for too long.

Turn to page 52.

You feel your heart pounding. You take a deep breath and brace yourself as the prow of your craft stops, balanced over the edge of the waterfall. Then, with stunning speed, you drop. You hear the roar of water all around you as you feel your kayak plummet, then a sudden jolt as it splashes down into the whirlpool below.

You feel the kayak start to whirl around and around. With alarm, you realize that you and your boat seem to be spiraling in ever-tighter circles, heading for the powerful vortex at the center of the pool. You're going to be sucked under!

"Paddle!" says a frantic voice. It's Vince, talking to you through your CB helmet.

You paddle with all your might. Slowly you feel the boat making progress. It really feels like your furious paddling is making a difference, but whether it is or not, you soon feel the boat break out of the whirlpool.

You sigh, gathering your wits, as the kayak moves downstream through a glassy section of water. Suddenly you hear a rumble from overhead. The blood drains from your face as you watch a giant boulder plunging crazily down the canyon, bouncing off the rock walls.

"Look out!" screams Vince.

Turn to page 46.

The next morning you have breakfast with Leslie, Sam, and Walter by the Daredevil Park Hotel pool.

"Which ride do you want to try first today?" Walter asks.

"That's easy," you say. "Just tell us which one is the most exciting. We'll do that one first."

"I'm with you," says Leslie. Sam can't talk through his mouthful of blueberry pancakes, but he nods with eager agreement.

"You've already ridden the rapids . . . that's one of our top adventures," Walter says. "In my opinion, the only rides that can match it for excitement are the Black Hole and Downhill Racer."

"The Black Hole—that's the roller coaster," says Leslie. "But what's Downhill Racer?"

"It's kind of like a souped-up, life-sized video game," Walter tells you. "You put on a pair of skis and take a lift to the top of a mountain. Then you race down to the bottom."

"But what if you can't ski?" asks Leslie.

Go on the the next page.

"It's all programmed with a very sophisticated system called Advanced Magnetic Remote Control," Walter answers. "You don't have to know how to ski, but you'll *feel* like you really can. The trip down the mountain is really exciting."

"I want to do that one first," says Leslie.

"I'd rather ride the roller coaster," says Sam.

Walter turns to you. "Looks like you're the deciding vote."

If you choose the Black Hole, turn to page 102.

*If you start with Downhill Racer,
turn to page 107.*

You run as fast as you can, hoping that the leopard is a robot and won't be able to chase after you. Reluctantly you look back, only to find that the leopard is still standing on the rocky ledge. It lets out another mighty roar, but this time you know for sure—it's fake.

With a sigh of relief, you head off toward the hotel. You can't be late for dinner, otherwise you're going to have to explain where you've been. But now that it's gotten darker, it's hard for you to move very fast. You look at your watch. It's five minutes to six. It would take a miracle for you to get back there on time.

Then, up ahead, you see what could be the miracle you've been looking for—the headlights of a jeep headed in your direction. If you could hitch a ride, you'd be back at the hotel in minutes. More than likely the driver is a Daredevil Park employee of some kind; chances are he couldn't care less what you're doing here.

Turn to page 65.

Rather than take any chances, you run as fast as you can up the stairs, then grope your way through the darkened mansion. Your hand finds a doorknob, and you breathe a sigh of relief when you turn it and the door opens to the outside.

You step out into a cluttered courtyard behind the mansion. As quietly as possible, you make your way over empty paint cans, scraps of lumber, and an occasional damaged ghoul robot. It seems to take forever to get through the rubble, but once you do, you run over to the bridge.

You don't hear any footsteps behind you, so you pause and look back. One by one lights are going on all over the mansion. You smile. While Dr. Bok is looking for you inside, you're about to escape.

The fog is so thick, you can only guess that Dr. Bok must have turned the fog machine up to "high." The bridge ahead of you seems to disappear completely after just a few feet. You look back once more, in time to see the front door open, and Dr. Bok running toward you, shouting angrily.

You start to run across the bridge, even though you can't see a thing. Suddenly your foot steps into a foggy void, and you plunge down.

Treading water, you look up at the bridge. About eight boards are missing—no doubt removed by Dr. Bok while you were floundering around in the courtyard earlier.

Turn to page 57.

The mansion appears to get bigger and bigger as you approach it. Standing in front of the gate, you can see that the building is run-down and about five stories high. All of the windows on the first three stories have been boarded up, and only a few of the windows on the top floor are lit.

Attached to each side of the building are two cylindrical towers that are even higher than the roof of the mansion, Extending from the gate is a cobblestone path that leads to the main entrance of the house. The path divides the front lawn, an unkept field of dirt with a few dead trees protruding from small patches of overgrown weeds. A feeling of death hangs in the misty air around this gloomy place. You wonder what awaits you inside.

Cautiously you step across a creaky wooden porch that leads to two black wooden doors. Mounted in the middle of each door is the brass head of a grinning gargoyle, a big ring held in its mouth. You decide to give one of them a try.

Bang, bang, bang. The knocker echoes inside as it strikes the brass plate behind the heavy ring. You wait for a moment, hoping that someone will answer the door, but instead a deep groaning voice says, *"Go away, if you value your life."*

Turn to page 42.

"You will see many fascinating sights as you travel into the heart of the jungle," intones the loudspeaker voice.

It's odd that the voice isn't saying anything about the approaching canoe, you think. The canoe is now close enough so that you can get a good look at its occupant—a young man who looks very much like the Amazon Indians you've seen in pictures. He's wearing very little clothing, but his face, arms, legs, and body are painted in orange and black slashes and swirls, and his straight black hair is crowned with a headdress made of brightly colored feathers.

You and your friends lean over the rail and watch as the Indian lashes his canoe to the side of the boat, scrambles on board, and then disappears into a cabin on the lower deck.

"But be warned!" says the voice from the loudspeaker. *"Savage Indians may try to attack our—"*

The voice stops abruptly. Then the low chugging of the boat's motor stops, too.

You, Leslie, and Sam look at each other uneasily.

"Something's definitely wrong," says Sam.

"Maybe we're *supposed* to think that," you say. "They always try to scare you on these rides."

"If that's the case," says Leslie, with a gulp, "it's working."

Go on to the next page.

You hear the sound of a scuffle and voices shouting below deck.

"C'mon," Sam says excitedly. "Let's see what's going on!"

"No way," says Leslie. "I'm staying right where I am."

You wonder what to do. You'd like to investigate below deck with Sam, but Leslie seems to think there's real danger down there. You look from one new friend to the other and try to make up your mind as the sounds of fierce fighting below grow louder.

If you decide to investigate, turn to page 23.

*If you choose to stay with Leslie,
turn to page 34.*

In spite of your fear, you're spellbound by this madman's performance. This guy is obviously a show-off in search of an audience—and you're his captive audience of one. If you can just let him know that you're interested in what he has to say, maybe somehow you can save yourself from a desperate situation.

Suddenly the doctor's mood swings again. Now he's defiant as he rises from his chair and strides over to the wall of television monitors.

"But tonight, I am back in command!" he says. "I have chosen Transylvania Island—my greatest creation—as the chief instrument of my revenge." To your horror, he reaches into a drawer and pulls out enough sticks of dynamite to blow all of Transylvania Island to smithereens. "I'm wiring this into the central computer. It's set to go off tomorrow afternoon."

You nod, and say in as respectful a tone as you can, *"Ehh ah-ah hah an eh-eh aw."*

Dr. Bok looks at you curiously. He obviously doesn't want to miss a compliment. He unties the gag. "What did you say?" he asks.

"Best haunted house I ever saw," you answer. "It would be a tragedy if I were the only kid in the world who ever got to see it."

Turn to page 50.

You feel a jolt as your kayak bounces off a huge rock, then a series of smaller jolts as it plunges down the white water. As the craft twists and turns every which way, thrashing its way through the water, you try to keep up with Vince's commands.

You use your paddle like a spear, pushing your kayak away from the sheer rock walls on either side of you, until a really vicious little whirlpool snatches it from your hands. All you can do now is cling to the sides of your kayak and hope for the best.

The kayak races on and on, following the twists and turns of the water. Your boat skips crazily, rounding bend after bend. You gasp as you realize that you're heading straight for a wall of rock!

"I want out of here!" you yell, just before you crash into the wall.

Turn to page 38.

Turn to page 35

Miss Wallace picks up the hand mike. "This is Jeanette Wallace, reporting to you from Daredevil Park, where we're about to apprehend the notorious Dr. Irving Bok," she says.

Dr. Bok looks stunned. As the two cameramen grab him, he's helpless to do much of anything. Miss Wallace flips out a badge. "We're undercover police officers. The press notified us immediately after they received your call. They knew you could be dangerous."

Dr. Bok glares at you. "You lied to me," he says.

"No," you say. "I really do think this is the best haunted house I've ever seen."

Turn to page 35.

Dr. Bok stands on one foot, then the other, trying to make up his mind.

"Otherwise you'll have no choice but to destroy your life's work beyond recognition, and what would that prove?" you say.

As Dr. Bok starts untying the ropes that bind you, you try to keep your hands from trembling. You've succeeded in flattering Dr. Bok into freeing you from your chair, but one false move could get you right back where you started.

Once your hands are free, you rub your arms to get the circulation going, then you reach for the phone.

Dr. Bok's hand comes down on yours. "What you say makes sense, but I'll do the phoning," he says.

In a few minutes, he's persuaded several people from the local newspapers and television station to come to his laboratory.

"See? They're dying for your story," you say, once he's finished. "Now why don't we tidy up a little while we're waiting for them to get here," you continue. "I'll put the rope back in the closet, and you can put away the dynamite."

Dr. Bok seems almost jolly as the two of you clean up. You manage to keep him talking about himself until you hear several vehicles pull up outside.

"They're here!" you say. "I'll go upstairs and get them."

"That won't be necessary," says Dr. Bok. "Watch this!"

Turn to page 59.

"What makes him so terrible?" you ask.

"I'm not sure exactly," Walter says with a sigh. "A couple of months ago he started acting funny. Until then everything had been fine. The Boks— Irving and Stanley—did everything together. Then Irving started claiming that every ride and each special effect was *his* invention. He started going too far—insisting on building rides that weren't really safe. Things got so out of hand, he had to be fired. Now he's bent on revenge."

"I guess his brother was pretty upset," you say.

"Stanley stuck by his brother," Walter says. "But he finally admitted that Irving was no longer himself. We tried to arrange for Stanley to stay, but since the Bok twins look and sound exactly alike, it was too easy for Irving to impersonate his brother and get inside the park. What's more, as one of the designers of Daredevil Park, he knows all the secret tunnels and entranceways into the place. He even built our security system, needless to say, so he knows how to get around that, too."

"What a mess," says Leslie.

"Hopefully, they'll have picked him up by—"

But Walter never gets to finish his sentence. The blue pickup truck is bearing down on all of you from behind, and the Bok brother behind the wheel is honking his horn, screaming, and shaking his fist.

"I think he wants to pass us," Leslie says.

Turn to page 4.

Telling yourself there's really nothing to worry about, you return Dr. Bok's smile. He may look sickly, but suddenly Dr. Bok moves surprisingly fast as he whips out a rope from behind his back and trusses you to the chair you're seated in.

"Hey!" you yell sharply, kicking your arms and legs in an effort to free yourself.

A handkerchief is pressed against your mouth. You shake your head violently from side to side, but Dr. Bok manages to tie it securely. In seconds, you're helpless—bound and gagged.

You have no idea what's going to happen to you next, but for some reason you're more angry than scared. First you let yourself be led into a trap, then you just sat there while this puny madman fumbled around in a closet for a rope to tie you up!

Thrashing around and trying to scream isn't going to do you any good, you decide. Discouraged, you slump back in your chair and sit silently.

You watch as Dr. Bok pushes a button on the master computer and one of the television monitors flashes on. You recognize the gloomy entrance hall to the mansion. Surprisingly, the suit of armor suddenly begins walking toward the camera.

Turn to page 29.

100

Walter leads you up several flights of stairs until you come to the top deck of the boat. Before you is a table with enough barbecued chicken, french fries, and chocolate brownies to feed a half dozen people. "Help yourselves. It's all for you," he says. "I'll be going now. Hope you survive the jungle. Good luck!"

Walter closes the door behind him, and the three of you look at each other feeling a little uneasy. At the same time you're very excited. You peer over the railing of the boat, but the fog is so thick you can't see a thing, so you go to work on the food instead. A few minutes later, a mighty blast from a foghorn sounds, and the boat glides forward.

Fifteen minutes later, you've polished off your third piece of chicken and started in on the brownies. The boat is moving faster now, but there's still nothing to look at—a thick shroud of fog makes it impossible to see even ten feet in front of you. You're beginning to think you're on the most boring ride in the world, when suddenly the fog evaporates, and Leslie lets out a gasp.

Sam's eyes are huge as he says, "Where are we?"

As if in answer, a man's voice booms out of a loudspeaker: *"Welcome to the most awesome wilderness on Earth—the Amazon rain forest!"*

Turn to page 26.

The official helps you to remove your helmet, and when he does, the crowd, the snow, and the racecourse disappear. It's hard to believe that the vivid sensations you've just experienced weren't real. Your whole body feels tired. In fact, your legs are shaking from exhaustion.

"That's because the magnetic remote was moving your body through the course in ways you're not used to," Walter explains, as he drives you and your friends over toward the roller coaster. "The effects are so realistic, people react by tensing their muscles. The Downhill Racer is so physically demanding, most of the people who come to Daredevil Park won't even be allowed to experience it. We're only letting people on the ski lift who are in top physical condition."

"But how are you going to know who qualifies?" Leslie asks.

"Simple," Walter says. "If you want to go downhill, you have to bring a note from your doctor. Fortunately the three of you checked out fine."

"I wondered why you required a signed medical evaluation before you'd accept us as winners," you say.

Turn to page 60.

The Black Hole doesn't really seem that different from a lot of other roller coasters you've been on—except that everything is bigger, steeper, and grander. You're seated in the front of the roller coaster, and Leslie and Sam are sitting together in the seat behind you. A Daredevil Park employee checks to make sure your restraints are properly secured.

Then comes the agonizingly slow climb to the top. You're filled with excitement and apprehension, wondering what kind of ride you're about to experience. When you're almost to the top, you crane your neck and look down. You're so far above the ground that the rest of Daredevil Park looks like a tiny scale model of an amusement park.

"I don't know about this," Leslie says uneasily.

"They wouldn't let us on unless it was safe," says Sam. "But I've been to Disneyland, Six Flags, and a bunch of other parks, and I've never seen anything that looks this wild."

You feel the roller coaster level off as you reach the top. "Here we go," you say softly, as the car noses its way over the crest.

The next four and a half minutes are as intense as any you've ever felt in your life. One minute you're weightless, the next minute you feel like you weigh a thousand pounds. The initial plunge, the twists, the loops and turns are all standard stuff. But because of its immense size, the Black Hole delivers about four times as much excitement as any ride you've ever been on.

Turn to page 28.

104

"I was just curious to see your house," you say honestly, looking around, hoping to flatter the guy. "It certainly is something." You hope that the smile you have forced onto your face is covering up the fear that's churning away inside of you.

"Well, since you're here, perhaps I'll allow you to look around." He fixes you with a menacing look. "But I must ask you a few questions. Are you alone?"

"Oh, yes," you say.

"And you got in here by—"

"Sneaking in," you confess.

"And you are—"

"One of the contest winners," you say, telling him your name.

"I am Dr. Bok, chief engineer of Daredevil Park," he says. "I am fine-tuning this exhibit, and I must get back to work. I should call the security guards, but I don't have time for any more interruptions. You can explore the house on your own, or you can come with me to the basement where I am working, whichever you like."

You'd like to finish exploring the mansion. However, it might be interesting to see what goes on behind the scenes, too.

If you choose to explore the mansion, turn to page 16.

If you go with Dr. Bok, turn to page 79.

"Don't interfere with what I'm doing and you won't get hurt," the Indian says, surprising you with his perfect English.

"Just what *are* you doing?" Sam asks.

"Protesting," he replies. "My name is Kayano, and I am an Amazon Indian. I'm also a junior at the University of New Mexico. I intend to stop Daredevil Park from exploiting my people."

"What do you mean?" you ask.

Kayano looks around the cabin of the boat. "This so-called Amazon Adventure portrays us Indians as a bunch of wild men who go around attacking innocent people. Nothing could be further from the truth."

You look at the burly Daredevil Park employee sitting slumped against the wall with his hands tied behind his back.

Kayano glares at you. "I didn't want to fight him," he says, pointing to a knife on the floor over by a chair, "but he pulled a knife. I had no choice."

"That voice from the loudspeaker did say we'd be attacked by savage Indians," says Leslie. "And that's certainly not a true picture of life in the Amazon. I know, I just read a really neat book about it."

You look at Leslie in amazement. A few minutes ago she was too scared to do anything. Now she's cool as ice.

"As far as I'm concerned, you're doing the right thing," she continues. "And with the press crawling all over the place, I'm sure the Daredevil Park management will be willing to listen to you."

Turn to page 31.

A half hour later you're standing at the top of the Downhill Racer ski run, your feet encased in ski boots, special ski gloves on your hands, and a high-tech helmet with a visor on your head. You can't be sure whether the ski run or the howling wind are real or the products of special effects.

You're looking with awe at the steep, snowy trail twisting down the mountain in front of you when the gate suddenly snaps open. You feel your head move down, your hands, holding ski poles, move ahead, and your whole body shoot forward so that you're careening rapidly down the slope.

You gasp. Surely you're going to lose your balance and fall! But instead, you feel your body move gracefully down the slope, magnetically controlled through your ski equipment.

At the top of the run the terrain is wide open, so you swoop back and forth, carving arcs in the snow, enjoying a feeling of perfect balance that you've never experienced before. It's as though you've instantly aquired expert skiing ability.

But you soon realize you're going to need all the expertise you can get. The terrain narrows and drops off sharply. You're going faster and faster, in powdered snow so deep you can't see through it any longer. Then, instead of soft powder, you're skiing on packed snow. You can feel your skis clattering over the ice.

Turn to page 78.

108

You decide to stay and play the video games, but first you check out your room. What a great sleep-over party you could have if all your friends were here. There's a huge bed, a sofa that converts into another bed, and a deluxe wide-screen TV with all those new video games built right in.

You flick the bathroom light on. It's about the size of your living room back home, with every surface covered in marble and mirrors. The bathtub is big enough to lie down in sideways and comes complete with a whirlpool. It'll feel good after a day of having your body flung about on the Daredevil Park rides, you think to yourself.

You bounce on the bed and play with the video games for a while. Then you think of an even better way to relax and watch TV.

You run some water in the tub and turn on the whirlpool. Then you pour in the little complimentary bottle of shampoo. You watch with satisfaction as the churning action of the water makes the bubbles build up fast.

You decide to move the television set into the bathroom. That way you can get the kind of close-up game play you like. But it'll take some doing. The TV is resting on a sturdy, built-in table. It's about four feet from the bathroom door, and it's facing the wrong way.

Turn to page 9.

As bad as things look now, I'm safer here than I would be if I tried to jump, you decide.

After a mile or so of jolting along the dirt path, you eventually come to the end of the forest. Bok stops the pickup where the pavement begins and looks around cautiously, like a wary animal about to run out from under cover.

"Won't be long now before we're there," he says.

Bok seems calmer now, so you figure it's okay to risk a little conversation. "Just where is it that we're going, Mr. Bok?" you ask.

Your innocent question puts him back into a rage. "It's *Doctor* Bok," he corrects you. "Do you think Daredevil Park could be the creation of an ordinary person? I hold advanced degrees in engineering, chemistry, and physics!"

"I didn't mean any disrespect, *Dr.* Bok," you say.

The doctor's eyes seem riveted to your face. "Everything I've achieved here is grounded in solid scientific theory." He sighs, exasperated. "But why waste time trying to explain things to a kid. Even my own brother thinks my inventions are dangerously flawed." He looks around again, making sure the coast is clear, then quickly starts down the road. "Kiddeeland," he says grimly.

"Pardon me?" you say.

"You wanted to know where we're going. We're going to the last place they'd look for me—the one place I had nothing to do with—Kiddeeland."

Turn to page 68.

Maybe if you can get the doctor talking, you can distract him long enough to grab the gun. You decide it's worth a try.

"Will it be a pleasant surprise?" you ask.

Dr. Bok winks at you. "If you like speed," he says.

"Oh, you're going to make it go faster," you say, trying to appease him. "Sounds like fun."

Dr. Bok's eyebrow twitches. "Fun?" he says. "Who said anything about fun!" As he screws the cover back on the control panel, he shakes with rage. "All you kids ever think about is fun!" He grabs you by the shoulders and shakes you back and forth.

You never thought it would be this easy. While Dr. Bok is shaking you, you pull the gun out of his belt and stick it in his stomach.

You take a step backward, still pointing the gun in his direction. "Outside," you say. You follow him out. "Dr. Bok, I think it's time you got a taste of your own medicine. Pick a horse."

"Oh, no," he says, with a gasp. "Not that."

You prod him over to a black horse. "Into the saddle," you say. Dr. Bok climbs up, then clings to the pole in front of the saddle, trembling. Without taking your eyes off Dr. Bok, you make your way back to the control panel and turn it on.

Turn to page 30.

Your arms feel heavy, like lead, but slowly—very slowly—you manage to move them into position to unhook your restraints. You wriggle free and take a deep breath, looking down at the ground about a hundred feet below.

There's nothing holding you now except the centrifugal force created by the spinning cage. As you inch your way around the side, you feel like you weigh five hundred pounds. The remote is only about six feet away from your outstretched hand, but it seems to take you forever—probably about four thousand spins and two hundred trips up and down the tower, you calculate as you creep toward your goal.

By the time you feel your hand touch the smooth metal of the remote, you're exhausted.

"I got it!" you scream, gripping it tightly. Too tightly, it turns out. You must have pressed a button, because as you inch your way back to your restraints, you can feel the cage spinning more and more slowly. You feel yourself coming unglued from the side of the cage. Desperately you grope for a handhold, a foothold, something! But it's too late! Nothing can keep you from plunging a hundred feet to the ground.

Too bad the cage was at the top of the tower when you accidently hit the button, otherwise you might have survived. As it is, there's now one less daredevil in this world.

The End

ABOUT THE AUTHORS

SARA COMPTON has created hundreds of songs and sketches for *Sesame Street* and other television shows and is the recipient of seven Emmy Awards. She is the author of *Stranded!* in the Skylark Choose Your Own Adventure series, as well as several books in the Earth Inspectors series.

SPENCER COMPTON is a student at the University of Colorado and has been doing exhaustive research for this book since the age of five.

ABOUT THE ILLUSTRATOR

FRANK BOLLE studied at Pratt Institute. He has worked as an illustrator for many national magazines and now creates and draws cartoons for magazines as well. He has also worked in advertising and children's educational materials and has drawn and collaborated on several newspaper comic strips, including *Annie* and *Winnie Winkle*. He has illustrated many books in the Choose Your Own Adventure series, most recently *The Lost Ninja, Kidnapped!, The Terrorist Trap, Ghost Train, Magic Master,* and *Master of Martial Arts.* He is also the illustrator of The Young Indiana Jones Chronicles series. A native of Brooklyn Heights, New York, Mr. Bolle now lives and works in Westport, Connecticut.

CHOOSE YOUR OWN ADVENTURE®